Dear Luke Ryan,

May this book bring you years of enjoyment.

Remember to "Always Be Kind"

Elaine Bamford

Elaine Bamford

To my grandchildren,
Cate, Will, Johnny, and Jack.

I strive daily to be
a good role model to each of you.

www.mascotbooks.com

A Cup of Loving Kindness

©2019 Elaine Bamford. All Rights Reserved. No part of this publication may be reproduced, stored in a retrieval system or transmitted in any form by any means electronic, mechanical, or photocopying, recording or otherwise without the permission of the author.

For more information, please contact:
Mascot Books
620 Herndon Parkway, Suite 320
Herndon, VA 20170
info@mascotbooks.com

Library of Congress Control Number: 2019904910

CPSIA Code: PRT0719A
ISBN-13: 978-1-64307-509-9

Printed in the United States

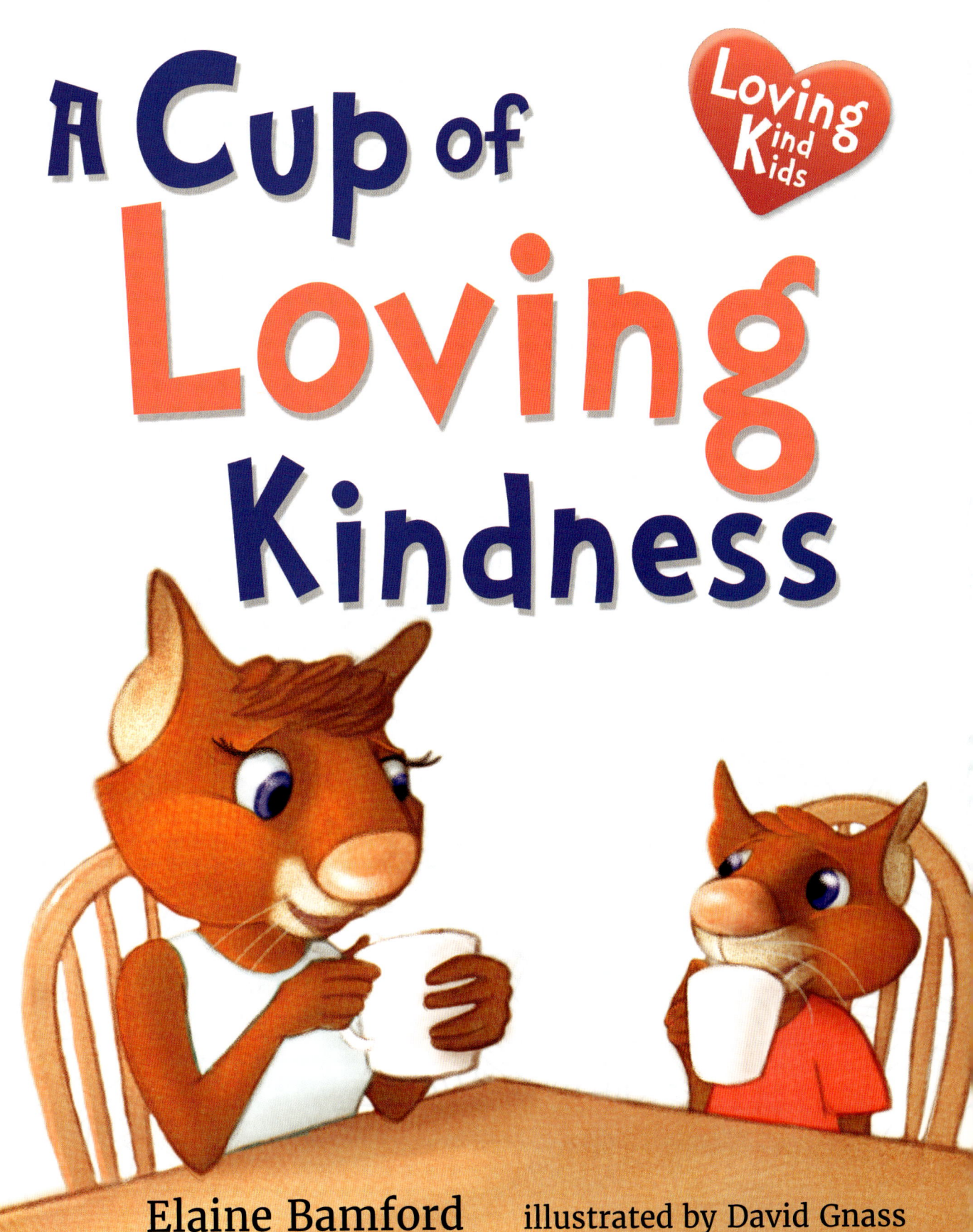

Everyone loved Sidney. He was such a helpful squirrel. His parents were so proud of him. Families were grateful when Sidney would offer to help.

However, Sidney didn't start off being loving and caring. Oh no, those who knew Sidney when he was younger knew the whole story.

In the past, his brothers and sisters would say, "Sidney, it is wonderful to share and be kind." His parents would tell him that he would enjoy school more if he would just be kinder to his classmates. His teacher would read stories that taught the children to be good friends, in hope that Sidney would hear the message. But Sidney didn't seem to listen or pay much attention to anyone else's feelings.

Sidney's mom would make herbal tea. Mom would always call these moments their cup of loving kindness talks. To him, it was just a great time to have his favorite tea. He just wasn't ready to get the message about love and caring for others.

Mom always finished their talks by saying, "One day Sidney, you will come to understand what it means to have loving kindness in your heart." She would smile and kiss him on the forehead, pat his shoulder and whisper, "One day."

His dad also tried. He would take Sidney for long walks and show him all the animals in the forest helping each other with open kind hearts. But Sidney wasn't ready. His dad would give him a big hug and say, "One day."

All that was about to change. A big storm was coming. All the families had prepared for the dangerous weather and were tucked in their burrows, hoping the storm would pass quickly.

As the wind picked up, Sidney's parents gathered the children. But where was Sidney? His dad called for him, but the wind was howling and the heavy rain had begun. The family was so scared and worried about Sidney.

As usual, Sidney had not listened to his parents. They told him to come home right after school, but Sidney was more interested in jumping across the wind-tossed tree limbs. He never even thought that his family might be worried.

By the time Sidney noticed how dark the sky was, it was too late to make it home. The heavy rain covered the forest. Sidney could not see a thing. He was cold, wet, and frightened. It was so dark that he got confused and lost his way. Luckily, he found shelter in a hollowed out fallen tree.

The next day when Sidney woke, he couldn't believe that he was in a cozy bed. He was not sure how he had gotten there but he was so happy to be safe, dry, and warm. When he looked up, he saw a lady in the doorway. She was smiling at him.

Mrs. Hedgehog was so happy to see him awake. She sat beside him and explained to Sidney that she found him while clearing away limbs and twigs that had fallen during the storm. He woke just long enough to tell her who he was but then fell back asleep. He was so exhausted from the storm, he slept almost the entire day.

Mr. and Mrs. Hedgehog sent their son, Jeremy, to neighboring forests to find Sidney's family. Sidney was worried that he would never see his parents again. However, the Hedgehog family was so kind and generous that it helped Sidney not to worry too much. They kept him warm and fed and even read bedtime stories to him. "Don't worry Sidney, your family will come to get you very soon."

He found out that other animals were also very caring. They brought extra food and clothing to the Hedgehog family because they had heard all about Sidney and wanted to help too.

Sidney couldn't believe how kind and loving they were to him. He remembered his mother having those talks about being kind to others. He was beginning to understand what his mom was trying to teach him.

One day, Mrs. Hedgehog heard Sidney crying. He was missing his family. Mrs. Hedgehog took Sidney by the hand and brought him to the kitchen where she gave him a warm cup of herbal tea. Sidney was so excited and told Mrs. Hedgehog that his mom gave him tea when they had their talks about being kind. Mrs. Hedgehog just smiled. He also explained that he felt sad because he hadn't listened like he should have during those special talks.

Surprisingly, Mrs. Hedgehog said the exact same thing as his mother—that one day, he would realize what loving kindness is all about. "Sidney, you know that loving kindness is a way of living your life. It means caring about others by being a good listener and offering a hand when you see that someone could use your help. I think you are already allowing kindness to enter your heart."

Sidney began to understand and thanked Mrs. Hedgehog and smiled. Just then there was a knock on the door.

It was Sidney's family! Jeremy had found them and explained what had happened. They were so grateful that Jeremy's family had taken care of Sidney. They had traveled all day to reach the Hedgehog family's home.

Mrs. Hedgehog offered them food and a place to sleep for the night. The next day they would be rested and ready to head back to their home.

As the Squirrel family was getting ready to leave, they couldn't believe their eyes. All the animal families had brought food for Sidney and his family's long trip home.

Sidney squeezed his mother's hand, stood on his tiptoes, and whispered in her ear, "Mom, I get it now."

"What, Sidney?" Mom asked.

"I understand about loving kindness. My heart is full of love and understanding. I am so sorry I haven't been a good listener. These families helped me understand what you were talking about. They didn't know me and yet they were so kind, and it made me feel so happy."

Sidney's mom bent down and gave him a big hug and a kiss on the forehead.

"I guess one day is today. I am so proud of you. Now you understand helping others makes your heart feel full and joyful."

That was the day Sidney changed. From that day on Sidney helped everyone. All the animals were so thankful for Sidney and his loving kindness.

As a special thank you, the Squirrel family invited the Hedgehog family for dinner. They had a wonderful time, sharing stories and laughter. After dinner they sat near the glow of the fireplace to keep warm. Each had a cup of herbal tea that Sidney had prepared. He was so proud to understand how caring for others could warm his own heart.

Sidney learned to show others loving kindness.

🌰 How would you describe loving kindness?

🌰 What happened to help Sidney learn about loving kindness?

🌰 Tell how someone has shown kindness to you.

🌰 Think of ways to show loving kindness to others.

Enrichment Activity

Writing Prompts

🌰 Think of a time when someone showed you loving kindness. Write about what that person did for you. Remember to tell how it made you feel.

🌰 Draw a picture that illustrates what loving kindness looks like to you.

About the Author

Being kind to others was a lesson taught to Elaine Bamford when she was very young by her own family. As a nurse, teacher, and caregiver, Ms. Bamford has learned what an impact the smallest gesture of kindness can make in the lives of others. For more than twenty years she taught students the importance of acts of kindness. There were always fundraisers for people in need, letters to our soldiers, and friendships with children from nearby preschool programs. The author's goal is to reinforce children's natural gift of kindness by writing stories that will appeal to the young mind and encourage a lifelong commitment to family and community with a strong sense of caring and kindness.

About the Illustrator

David Gnass specializes in children's book illustrations. Residing in Kingston, Ontario, he has illustrated many children's books with all the passion and love that was sparked years before when he drew his first illustrations as a child.